DATE DUE

THE TIME OF
THE FOREST

TOM McGOWEN

Houghton Mifflin Company
Boston   1988

1   S

To my friend, Harry Snowden, Jr.

Library of Congress Cataloging-in-Publication Data

McGowen, Tom.
The time of the forest.

Summary: When war breaks out between their opposing
sides in ancient Denmark, Bright Dawn of the farming
community and Wolf of the hunters' tribe flee from
the battle and take refuge in the forest.
1. Denmark—History—To 1241—Juvenile fiction.
[1. Denmark—History—To 1241—Fiction. 2. War—
Fiction] I. Title.
PZ7.M16947Ti 1988   [Fic]   87-26191
ISBN 0-395-44471-3

Printed in the United States of America

S   10 9 8 7 6 5 4 3 2 1

PROLOGUE

Five thousand years ago, in the land which one day would become known as Denmark, a forest covered the earth for tens of thousands of square miles, a seemingly endless array of oak, elm, and linden trees, growing so closely together that their leafy branches formed a continuous shaggy roof overhead. Beneath this vast canopy, the forest floor was shrouded in green gloom and shadows into which shafts of pale sunlight filtered down here and there through gaps in the foliage. Through this spectacular wilderness wandered herds of deer, packs of wolves, families of wild pigs, solitary bears and wolverines, and an incredible profusion of other animal and bird life. Golden-orange salmon flickered through the streams that wound through these woods, and silver-and-black-speckled trout and

1

other fish stocked the lakes and ponds around which the forest spread.

Widely scattered throughout the vast forest were small tribal groups of humans, seldom coming in contact with one another, and often regarding themselves as the only people in a world that consisted solely of the forest. They were hunter-gatherers, who moved their skin-tent communities from place to place throughout a year, following the movement of the deer, which were their main prey, and gathering the natural harvest of herbs, roots, fruit, nuts, and other bounty that had accumulated in each place since their last visit. This was the way of life their ancestors had followed for thousands of years. The forest was their home and their livelihood.

But moving up from the south toward the forest were scattered groups of a different people. Their way of life was agriculture — the planting and harvesting of grain and the breeding of small herds of goats and oxen — but they had been forced out of their ancestral homeland on distant plains by drought. Moving northward over many months in a search for new land, they had reached the barrier of the forest and had realized that the moisture and rich soil that enabled these trees to thrive would nurture their plants as well. They attacked the forest, cutting down and burning out great sections of it to make room for their fields, and they built small, permanent settlements of huts made of stone and turf, or longhouses made of logs. To them the forest was frightening — its creatures were enemies — and they were determined to conquer it to fit their needs. Thus, their way of life, their outlook, their very thoughts, were completely different from those of the people who dwelt within the forest.

It was inevitable that, sooner or later, these two would come face to face.

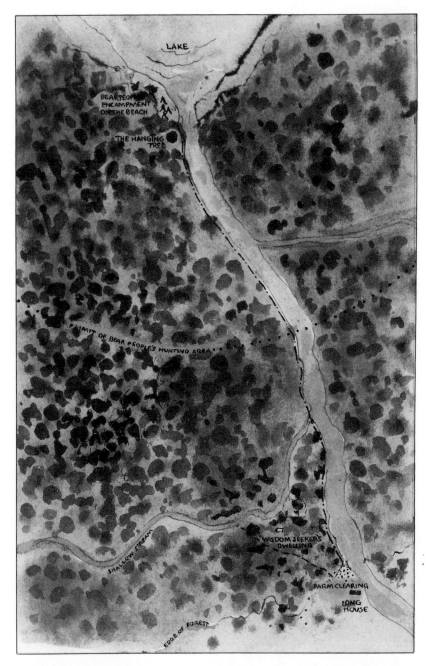

LAKE

BEAR PEOPLE'S
ENCAMPMENT
ON THE BEACH

THE HANGING
TREE

LIMIT OF BEAR PEOPLE'S HUNTING AREA

SHALLOW STREAM

WISDOM SEEKER'S
DWELLING

FARM CLEARING

LONG
HOUSE

EDGE OF FOREST

PLOUGHMAKER AND STARWATCHER'S
ROUTE ALONG THE RIVER —·—·—·.

ROUTE OF WOLF AND
BRIGHT DAWN — — —

1

The oak tree was a gray and gnarled forest patriarch that numbered its age in centuries. Its trunk was so massive that a man trying to put his arms around it would have left a gap a full arm's length between fingertips. Its lower branches were stout, twisted columns that writhed upward like the thick groping tentacles of a sea beast.

From one of them dangled the body of a hanged man.

He was naked, but a hood of leather covered his entire head. His hands were loosely tied behind his back with a leather thong, and several thongs, tightly knotted together, formed the rope, one end of which was looped around the branch and the other pulled into a noose around his neck. He had obviously been hanging there for some time, for the flesh of his body had largely dried and shrunk away, and his skin was stretched tightly over the bones. Beneath the hood, his face was little more than a parchment-covered skull with shadowed hollows where life-filled eyes had once looked upon the world. He had been known as Fish Brother because of his swimming ability, and he had gladly let the people of his tribe hang him as a sacrifice to the Horned One, the god of the forest, who helped hunters.

The tree from which Fish Brother's body hung stood in the center of a small clearing beside the bank of a narrow stream that ran through a portion of the immense forest. A few hundred paces from the clearing, two men were winding their way in and out among the close-growing trees that clustered along the stream's bank. Both men were dark-eyed with dark hair and beards and olive-tinted skin. They were dressed alike in sleeveless knee-length smocks and moccasinlike footwear made of smoke-darkened oxhide stitched with animal tendon "thread." Each man had several leather bags hanging by thongs from his shoulder, and each carried a stout-shafted spear with a sharp-edged point of flint chipped into a smooth laurel-leaf shape.

The men clutched these spears as if they expected to have to use them at any moment. Their faces were grim, and they cast nervous glances into the gray-green maze of trunks and leaf-littered ground that seemed to extend away endlessly from the bank of the stream. They were intruders in this forest, and they found it strange and frightening.

"I cannot bear the thought of another day in this place," muttered the younger of the two, whose name was Starwatcher. He spoke in a near whisper, as they had both fallen into the habit of doing since they had come into the forest. "Can we not turn back now, Ploughmaker?"

The other gave a quick shake of his head. "No. The Wise Ones charged us to go as far as we could. We have enough food left for six days, so we shall keep going for one more day, and tomorrow we can start the five-day journey back."

Starwatcher groaned. "The Mother's curse on this place! I keep expecting some savage beast to leap upon us, or some dark spirit to come creeping out of the gloom! I have heard terrible sounds at night while I've been on watch, Ploughmaker. And I have seen shining eyes watching us out of the darkness!"

"I, too," Ploughmaker told him. "But we have been kept safe. The Mother is watching over us."

"Praise to her," intoned Starwatcher, and fell silent.

Having come to the forest after many months of

migration, the People, the tribe of farmers to which Ploughmaker and Starwatcher belonged, had decided they could make a new home at the forest's edge. But they feared what might be within the dark, menacing woods that loomed over them. They must discover whether they would be completely safe living in the forest's shadow. So Ploughmaker and Starwatcher had been sent to explore by the Wise Ones, the three women who governed the People. The two men had been moving through the forest for four days, following the stream that would lead them back out again.

"I am hungry," said Starwatcher after a time. "It must be nearly midday. Can we not —" He broke off abruptly, for at that moment they stepped into the clearing and beheld the hanging man. They froze in their tracks, staring with shock and horror.

"Mother protect us!" exclaimed Ploughmaker, making the sign to ward off evil. "It's a man! There must be people in here. People!" The possibility of encountering other humans in this place had never entered his mind, nor that of his companion.

"Why is he hanging there?" quavered Starwatcher. "Who would have done that to him?"

The other man licked his lips, staring. "I think it must be some kind of magic," he said fearfully. He glanced about, noting the even circular shape of the clearing, with the solitary ancient tree in its exact center. "There is a feeling of magic about this place!"

Suddenly Starwatcher's head jerked in surprise; his eyes widened. "Listen!" he hissed.

Ploughmaker stared at him for a split second, then froze, straining to hear what his companion heard. After a few moments, faint as a whisper from the direction toward which they were heading, came a repetition of the sound that had alerted the younger man. It was the unmistakable sound of the shrill voices of children, raised in excitement.

The two men regarded each other with shocked eyes. To hear such a sound in the midst of this endless wilderness was astonishing, but to hear it while confronted by a shriveled, dangling corpse was horrifying. Starwatcher wavered, fighting the impulse to turn and run.

Ploughmaker thrust out a hand to hold the younger man back. "Hold! We must see what this is," he declared with firmness. "We must find out — for the good of the People."

"We'll have to — go past *that!*" objected Starwatcher, with a gesture toward the hanging corpse.

"Then we'll have to go past it," said the other. "Come."

They moved forward slowly along the edge of the

clearing, giving the tree wide berth and eyeing the gaunt corpse nervously. When they were well past it, both men took deep breaths of relief. They left the clearing and moved on cautiously through the trees, always keeping the riverbank in sight. After several hundred paces they observed an increasing brightness ahead, and after about another hundred paces they saw that the forest abruptly ended. Ploughmaker dropped to all fours and scrambled forward a ways, then sank flat against the ground and wormed his way ahead until he could peer over a broad, gnarled tree root. Starwatcher followed suit. Side by side at the forest's edge they stared at what lay before them.

It was a large natural clearing, in the middle of which was a small lake into which flowed the stream they had been following. From the edge of the forest a grassy, boulder-dotted expanse sloped gradually downward to merge with a white sand beach that stretched another hundred paces or so to the lake. The section of beach directly in front of the two men was dotted with some dozen conical tents made of tanned animal skins that had been sewn together with strips of leather and fitted over tripods of stripped saplings. Among these tents a number of people were busy at various tasks.

Most of the workers were women, and there was a

generous sprinkling of children, but no young men were to be seen. A group of women sat together in a circle on the sand, their legs stretched straight out, their laps filled with hides they were sewing together with slim needles of bone and thin strips of sinew. Nearby, two girls worked at cleaning the last bits of fat and muscle from another hide; one held it stretched flat on the ground while the other scraped it vigorously with a sharp piece of flint. It was a scene such as Ploughmaker and Starwatcher might have seen among their own people at times, and they found this rather surprising. Out in the water of the lake, knee-deep, some of the older children, girls and boys, were fishing with nets made of dried woven grass and fish spears with barbed heads of carved bone. It was one of the shouts of triumph from these youngsters that Ploughmaker and Starwatcher had heard.

The women were dressed alike in sleeveless garments of some golden-brown hide; they reached to midcalf and were trimmed with fringes of knotted rawhide strips. Some of the older girls were dressed like the women, but most of the younger children wore only skimpy apronlike flaps of leather held in place by a thong around the waist, or they were naked. To the two men, all these women and children looked alike; they all had pale yellow hair, their cheekbones were high,

11

and their noses were thin and slightly hooked. Their eyes, which were actually blue or gray, seemed oddly colorless to Ploughmaker and Starwatcher. The two men wondered whether these bright-haired creatures were truly human. There had never been such hair or eyes among the People.

"They are all women," murmured Starwatcher. "A tribe of women-things, Ploughmaker!"

"No. There are men-children among them," the older man pointed out. "Men-children grow to be men. The grown men must be somewhere else."

They were silent for a time. Then Starwatcher said, "What shall we do?"

"Wait. We must wait to see what the men are like. We must be able to tell the Wise Ones as much as we can about these — these people."

They continued to watch, carefully changing their positions from time to time when they grew uncomfortable. The sun crept lower in the sky.

Abruptly there was a stir on the beach. The women were gazing off toward another part of the forest, and several of them began to run in that direction. A handful of the children who had been fishing came splashing out of the water and pelted after the women.

A small group of fair-haired, pale-eyed men had emerged from the forest. They wore shirtlike garments and leg coverings stuffed into knee-high boots of soft leather. All carried bows and had bark quivers of arrows slung over their shoulders. Two of the men carried a long stout pole, one end resting on each man's shoulder. A dead stag, its feet lashed to the pole with rawhide thongs, hung head down between them. There were calls of greeting between the men and the women who had come to meet them.

"Hunters!" said Starwatcher in a voice at the edge of a whisper. "They are hunters — like wild animals!"

"Come. We must go," breathed Ploughmaker. He realized that other men of these hunter people must still be out hunting and might return at any time and from any part of the forest — perhaps from the very part where he and Starwatcher lay hidden. They had best leave this place quickly.

Carefully the two of them slid backward until they were well out of view from the beach. Then they rose and trotted, half crouching, until they had put several hundred paces between themselves and the forest edge. They hunkered down, their heads nearly touching.

"What are your thoughts on this, Ploughmaker?" whispered Starwatcher.

"That they are but five days' journey from where we shall be ploughing our fields," said the older man grimly. "Some day, some of them might come upon our dwelling place as we came upon theirs. I will not be able to sleep well, thinking of that!"

Starwatcher's face took on a look of concern. "Do you not think we could be friends with them?"

"They are hunters," Ploughmaker told him in a bleak voice. "They are not like us. They live by killing, like wild animals, as you said — like wolves or foxes or any of the hunting animals that live in this forest. We could not be friends with such creatures!"

"I suppose not," admitted Starwatcher after a moment, thinking of the strange appearance of the hunter people. "They probably do not even worship the Mother."

Ploughmaker snorted. "They probably worship the tree that dead man is hanging from!" He glanced about sharply. "Come, let us get away from here. The sooner the Wise Ones know of this, the sooner they can decide what must be done." He scurried toward the riverbank, Starwatcher at his heels, both men still staying low to keep from being seen.

But they had been seen. Some thirty paces from where they had crouched, talking, stood two boys of the hunter tribe, frozen in the shadows in the way that was second nature to them. They had been making their way to the beach, carrying the birds they had brought down with their arrows, when they caught sight of the two strangers. They watched the two men with wide-eyed astonishment, as amazed at the sight of humans who were not members of their tribe as the two farmers had been to encounter other people. Now, as Ploughmaker and Starwatcher moved out of sight and the sounds of their movement (noisy to the ears of the young hunters) died away in the distance, the boys turned to stare at each other. They were about the same age; some fourteen or fifteen years.

"'What were they?" whispered one.

"Men," said the other. Then, uncertainly, he added, "I *think*. They looked like men. They must be from another tribe." He had heard, from his tribe's elders, that there were other groups of hunters in the forest. It was said that, many fingers of years ago, his tribe, the Bear People, had encountered another tribe and there had even been an exchange of some of the young women; a few girls of each tribe had chosen to stay with young men of the other. He didn't know if this was true or not.

His companion was scowling. "They should not be in our hunting place," he declared. "They will take what is ours! What shall we do, Wolf?"

The boy called Wolf considered rapidly. Boarfighter, the chief, would have to be told about these strangers, and Wolf's first inclination was to rush back at once with the news. But it occurred to him that it might be well to find out more about the strangers — where they were camped and how many more of them there might be.

"Go tell Boarfighter what we have seen," he told his friend. "I will follow after those two men and see what I can learn of them. I will leave a trail for you, Fleetrunner."

The other nodded. "May the Horned One guide you, Wolf," he said. Then he turned and glided off among the trees.

Wolf moved to where the two men had crouched, peered about, and sighted the spoor that led toward the riverbank. In quick-footed silence, he began to follow it.

and come after them. As was his people's custom, Wolf stretched out a hand in a sign of homage to Fish Brother as he passed the body. Fish Brother had given himself to the Horned One so that the Bear People would have good hunting for another year. Wolf knew that the man had been well repaid. He was now a member of the Horned One's hunting band and would live happily in the sky forever.

When the two men made camp for the night, Wolf watched their fire-starting method with astonishment. His own people used fire drills, small bows with which a pointed stick was spun among kindling until the friction caused a blaze. Instead, one of these men laboriously twirled a stick between the palms of his hands. Wolf also watched as they prepared a meal for themselves. They removed handfuls of grain from the bags they carried, mixed it with a bit of water from the river, and slapped a dollop of this paste onto a flat rock heated in the fire, to produce a lumpy sort of pancake. The boy could not understand all the things they were doing and couldn't imagine what they were eating. He suspected it might be some kind of magical food. It certainly didn't seem to be any kind of animal flesh.

He was equally puzzled about their preparations for the night. Ploughmaker and Starwatcher had worked out a system whereby one slept for half a night while the other kept watch. One man curled up to sleep while the other sat, tending the fire and peering into the darkness, clutching his spear. Why didn't they both lie down and go to sleep? wondered the boy. What could they be so afraid of? After a time he shrugged, stretched out with a tree at his back, and quickly dropped off to sleep.

In the morning he let his quarry start off and then refreshed himself with a quick swim in the stream. Leaving the water, he pulled on his clothing, picked up his bow, and resumed the chase. His sharp eyes and knowledge of the woods enabled him to feed himself as he went, with a handful of mushrooms here, some eggs from a bird's nest there, and a cluster of tasty roots of cattails pulled from beside the stream. From time to time as he moved along he made a quick gash with his knife in the bark of a tree or bent a slim young sapling over so that it pointed in the direction he was heading. These were signs to show which way he had gone. Fleetrunner or anyone else coming after him would notice them at once.

Several days later, in the early morning, the boy saw the two men he was following suddenly become more sure of themselves and less fearful. A brightness ahead told Wolf that they were approaching a clearing, and abruptly the two men broke into a run. Wolf began to move more cautiously. Presently he was peering from behind a tree at the forest's edge, trying to understand these new sights and impressions.

Wolf had always known that the forest came to an end, for other members of his tribe had seen it, but he had pictured it as a sort of clearing with a wall of trees around it, like the clearings his people camped in. He was shocked and dazzled by the vast, open brightness that seemed to extend into an endless distance. He felt as if he were at the very edge of the world, and he clutched at a tree trunk to keep from falling forward into the terrible void that confronted him!

After a time, he began to take notice of what lay nearer to him. A broad half-circle nearly a mile wide had been cut out of the forest where the stream entered it; hundreds of trees had been chopped down and their stumps burned to the ground. A structure made of trimmed logs stood near the stream, and fences of split logs formed pens. In one, a dozen small, furred, horned animals ambled about, while in another, six large creatures resembling forest bison stood chewing at something. At the river, in the pens, and in the bare, open field, strangely clad dark-haired people were busy at tasks that were completely puzzling to Wolf. As the two men he had been trailing burst out of the forest they yelled to attract attention, and soon they were the center of a cluster of people. Wolf watched as the two made their way to the log structure and entered it, then he squatted down at the base of the tree and tried to make sense out of what he was seeing.

He was shocked and angered by the damage that had been done to the forest; it did not seem right for anyone to do such a thing, and he felt that the Horned One would be enraged by it. He could not imagine why the dark-haired people would have wanted to make an open area in the woods; didn't they have enough of it in all that vast openness that lay beyond?

He was amazed by the penned animals. They were new to him, and he could not imagine how the dark-haired people had managed to capture them. He was even more amazed when a handful of the dark-haired children went to the pens and let the animals out. Instead of running away or attacking the young humans, the creatures calmly allowed themselves to be chivvied along to the edge of the forest where they began to graze on the sparse grass that grew there. The idea of a tame animal was completely unknown

3

"What was it like in there, Ploughmaker?"

"Did you meet any danger?"

"Did you see any ghosts?"

An excited chatter of questions swirled around Ploughmaker and Starwatcher as they made their way to the longhouse in the midst of the crowd that had swarmed to meet them when they came out of the forest. Starwatcher grinned and strutted slightly at all this attention, but Ploughmaker kept his face expressionless. "You will hear all about it when we tell the Wise Ones" was all he would say.

They entered the longhouse, trailed by the crowd, and made their way down the narrow hallway between the rows of little cubicles formed of wooden-pole walls with hanging mats of woven straw for doors, where people slept and kept their belongings. The floor was bare earth, broken at regular intervals with shallow pits lined with stones, in which fires for cooking were made and shared by the owners of the cubicles on either side of a pit. At the far end of the longhouse was an open area where the People held meetings and conducted religious rituals, and it was here that the Wise Ones were waiting — three women seated cross-legged on the thick covering of dried rushes which had been spread over the dirt floor.

One was an elderly white-haired woman whose face was a mask of fine wrinkles from a lifetime spent in the fields beneath a hot sun. Another was a girl of about fourteen. The third was a plump, pleasant-faced matron of middle years, her dark hair just beginning to gray. These were the three holy women who ruled the tribe in the name of the goddess known as the Mother.

"It is good to see you safely back," the middle-aged woman said, smiling. "Well, what did you find? Can we make a life there in peace and safety, or is there danger?"

Starwatcher glanced quickly at Ploughmaker as if wondering how he would answer. Ploughmaker hesi-tated, then said, "Yes, Cloud-of-Summer — there is danger."

The smiles vanished from the faces of the three

women, and the whispers and rustlings of the crowd in the longhouse grew still. "Speak," said Cloud-of-Summer, the middle-aged woman, her eyes intent upon Ploughmaker.

"There are people — or things *like* people — living in there," he said, and there was a gasp from the listeners behind him. "They look like people, but they have pale skin, pale eyes, and hair the color of straw. They live by hunting! We saw some of them bringing in the bodies of dead animals and birds. They live beside a lake among all the trees, no more than five days' journey from here."

There was complete silence. The white-haired woman leaned forward. "Did you have any dealings with them? Did you talk to them?"

Ploughmaker shook his head. "No, Snow Walker, we kept hidden. I did not want to let them know of us. They might have killed us! There was a dead man hanging from a tree near their dwelling place. We think they killed him and hanged him there for some magic. They might have done the same to us! There is no way to tell what such ones might do. They are not like us in any way!"

Cloud-of-Summer looked thoughtful. "This does not sound good to my ears. What if they find out about us? What if they come here? What might they do?"

Ploughmaker nodded sharply. "That is my thought, too. They are hunters — what if they try to hunt *us*?" A hiss of shocked whispers passed through the crowd.

"We must keep watch for them so that they cannot catch us unaware," suggested the girl who was the youngest of the Wise Ones. The other two nodded.

"Yes, that is what we must do, Blossom," agreed Cloud-of-Summer. "We must have someone watching the forest at all times during the day, and someone awake and listening all night. We shall take turns at this, all of us." She glanced toward a corner, where three furry shapes lay. "We can depend on the dogs to help, too. They bark at strange smells. This can help warn us."

"But watching is not enough," said the eldest Wise One grimly. "We must be prepared to fight these creatures — all of us!"

Cloud-of-Summer sighed. "You speak truly, Snow Walker. We must be ready to fight, indeed." Her eyes swept the cluster of dark-haired people. "Do you hear this, People of the Mother? You must be prepared to seize a weapon and fight with it at any moment of day or night. My sisters and I will work out a way whereby all can share in standing watch against these ones who may be our enemies. If they do come against us, we shall be ready for them!"

4

Wolf continued to watch the dark-haired people for the next few days, taking time out only to go deeper into the woods to hunt for food. He still could not understand most of the things the dark-haired ones were doing, but he began to realize that they were all working as hard at the things they did as his people worked at hunting and gathering. Somehow that made the strangers seem more like true people to him. For the most part, they all looked alike to him, but he was beginning to recognize a few of them. He had come to know the features of the two men he had trailed; there was another man he could pick out because of his limp; and there was a portly, gray-haired woman who seemed to spend most of her time telling groups of the others what to do.

There was also a girl about his own age or a bit

younger. She had midnight-black hair, she seemed to laugh a lot, and her dark-eyed face, even at a distance, was oddly attractive to the boy. He wondered what her name might be and what she would be like to talk to.

He no longer quite knew what to make of the dark-haired people. They were certainly intruders, and they had done injury to part of the forest, but he could see that they weren't hunters and had no interest in going into the forest. Wolf no longer felt they were a threat to his tribe's well-being. He wondered how they got their food; it still seemed to him that magic must be involved. It would be a very useful thing to know how they did it! He began to wish that he could simply *ask* them about their strange way of life. What if he were to just walk out of the woods toward them with his hands in the air to show that he had no weapons and meant no harm? Would they accept such a gesture of friendship and talk with him — or would he get a spear in his belly?

He wished for some way to make contact with them. If only one of them would come into the woods alone — that girl, for example. He felt that he could talk to her. If only she would come into the woods, he thought.

And the next day, almost as if the Horned One had arranged it, she did.

He was watching as she took the group of small horned animals out of their pen and guided them to a grassy part of the field near the edge of the woods. They were headed straight toward his hiding place, and as they neared, he heard for the first time the strange, quavering baaing noise they made, which sounded funny to him and made him grin. They fanned out and began to graze, and the girl knelt down gracefully and composed herself to keep watch over them. From time to time she darted a sharp glance toward the forest, no more than fifty paces away.

After a time, Wolf saw that one of the creatures was straying away from the others, coming quite close to the forest. The girl noticed it, too. She called out to it but was ignored. Scrambling to her feet, she darted after it. It baaed loudly and, like a naughty child, turned and trotted quickly into the woods.

It was certainly no forest animal, thought Wolf, for it paid no attention to where it was going. It came trotting straight toward his hiding place. Had he been the animal he was named for, it would have become his prey in an instant. As it was, he took one step, stooped, and scooped up the startled creature as it came past him, gripping it tightly so that it couldn't kick him with its sharp little hoofs. Stepping back into his hiding place, he looked toward the girl.

She hadn't seen him, he knew, because he was well screened by thick tangles of leafy branches, but she was staring with dismay toward where the animal had entered the forest. She glanced over her shoulder, but the nearest of her people was too far distant to have noticed what had happened. She turned back to the forest and seemed to make up her mind. Drawing a deep breath, she hurried into the trees after the runaway animal. With a surge of delight, Wolf realized that his wish had come true.

The girl's name was Bright Dawn, and the instant she entered the edge of the forest she stopped dead, staring about in apprehension. It seemed to her that she had stepped into another world. The green gloom that she suddenly found herself facing was like a menacing living thing. Again she glanced over her shoulder to assure herself that the open field was still behind her, easily reached with a quick scurry if necessary. Then she faced the forest once more, gathering her courage, and began to look about for the goat.

Wolf watched her curiously. It was obvious that she was afraid of something, just as the two men he had trailed had been, but he still didn't know what caused that fear. Now that he was about to come face to face with her, he found that he was just a bit afraid himself. Quickly he stepped out of his hiding place, no more than a few paces from her, and held out the goat. He licked his lips nervously and tried to smile. "Here it is," he told her. "I caught it for you." It did not occur to him that she might not understand his words.

Bright Dawn froze, and a tiny squeak of terror slipped between her lips. It seemed to her that he had materialized out of thin air, as if he were a ghost or a demon about to kill her in some hideous way. Then, as he simply stood there, smiling and holding the goat toward her, she collected her wits and looked at him more closely. He was human after all. It came to her that he must be one of the forest people.

She had listened with the others as Ploughmaker had told the Wise Ones of the pale forest dwellers that were more like hunting animals than humans, and she had formed a picture in her mind of gaunt, snowy-skinned, wild-eyed *things* that only remotely resembled people. But this one that now stood only a few paces away from her didn't fit that picture at all. It — he — seemed to be a boy of about her own age, a head taller than she, and much like her people except for his odd coloring. His face was a perfectly human, boyish face; rather nice-looking in an odd way, she decided, despite the thin, bent nose and those pale eyes. And he was definitely smiling, as if he wanted to be friends, holding the goat out toward her. Of course, this *could* be a trick — but if he had wanted to hurt her he could have just leaped on her the instant she came among the trees.

Wolf was considering the girl. Now that he was close to her he could see that her eyes were a deep brown color — like the rich fur of the brown bear that was his tribe's totem, he thought with delight. In his mind, he compared her features with those of the girls of his people. She *was* different. Her dark eyebrows formed interesting curves above her eyes, her nose was wider and straighter than the noses of his people, her lips seemed fuller and redder. But all these differences added up to a face that he found very pleasant.

He wondered why she hadn't replied, then suddenly realized that she was probably frightened. After all, he had been watching her for some time, but she hadn't even known that he existed, and then he had popped out at her unexpectedly.

He held the goat out until it was nearly touching her. "Don't be afraid," he begged, still smiling. "Take your beast."

Her eyes never leaving his face, she lifted trembling hands and clutched the animal to her chest. She stared at Wolf a moment more, then whirled and darted out of the trees into the open field.

Wolf watched as she hurriedly gathered the horned

animals together and shooed them back to their pen. He had hoped that he and the girl might talk for a while, but she was obviously afraid of him. Well, it was a beginning, anyway, he thought, squatting down among the trees at the forest's edge. Surely she would tell her people of him and how he had caught the runaway horned creature for her, and now that they knew he meant no harm, they might try to make contact with him. Perhaps in another day or so he would finally be talking with them and learning about them. And perhaps the girl would have lost her fear of him.

He was turning this pleasant fantasy over in his mind when something plucked at his attention. It was the sound of a crow making three loud caws, pausing a moment, then cawing twice more. But Wolf knew it was not really a crow; it was a signal he and Fleetrunner often used to locate each other in the woods. Fleetrunner must have followed his trail and was now nearby, seeking him.

Wolf moved farther into the forest and answered the signal. Within a short time Fleetrunner appeared, but he was not alone. To Wolf's surprise, a number of hunters were with him. One of them was Foaming Mouth Bear, Boarfighter's son, who generally acted as his father's second-in-command. He strode up to Wolf and clapped him on the shoulder.

"It was wise of you to follow the strange men to their camp, Wolf," he commended the boy. He was a rangy man of about twenty, half a head taller than Wolf, who grinned at the compliment.

"What are they like, Wolf?" asked a hunter named Badger Fears Nothing. "Fleetrunner says they have hair the color of night! Is this true?"

"It is true," Wolf assured him, thinking for just a moment of the black cloud that framed the stranger-girl's face. "But they seem to be people much like the Bear People in other ways."

Foaming Mouth Bear gave him an odd look, then jerked his head toward the glimmer of daylight, bright between the trees, that marked the edge of the forest. "Lies their camp yonder?" he asked.

Wolf nodded, and the man turned toward the others. "Spread out and let us look these strangers over," he ordered. "Let us try to get an idea of their number."

Wolf accompanied them to the forest edge. Crouching behind trees and bushes, the hunters studied the dark-haired people with as much amazement and curiosity as Wolf had felt the first time he watched them. A number of the dark-haired men were gathered in the open field, bent down over some of the long gashes they had put into the earth with an odd contrivance made of wooden stakes pulled by a pair of the large horned animals.

"What are they doing?" murmured Fleetrunner, who lay alongside Wolf, peering over a tree root.

"I have not been able to tell," Wolf whispered back. "They are either taking something out of the ground or putting something into it, I think."

"Putting something into the ground?" said Fleetrunner. He stifled laughter at the thought of such silliness.

After a long time, Foaming Mouth Bear gave the call of a hawfinch, a signal to the hunters to gather with their leader. Wolf and the others left the line of trees and at some distance into the forest squatted in a circle with Foaming Mouth Bear in the center.

He gave a shake of his head. "They are nothing like us," he said in a voice that sounded faintly shocked. "I do not think they are even real people! I think they may have come from beyond the edge of the world, from the open sky!" Several of the hunters opened their eyes wide to show their astonishment at these words.

Foaming Mouth Bear seemed to reflect for a moment. "I make them out to be no more than two hands of men, three of women, a little less than two of children," he said. There was a general mutter of agreement from the others, and he nodded. "Then I think there are enough of us here to do what we agreed must be done."

Wolf frowned, not understanding. "Of what do you speak, Foaming Mouth Bear?"

The man's eyes swung to him. "On the way here we spoke much about this, Wolf. We took counsel among ourselves about what we should do concerning these strangers. We agreed that we cannot allow them to come into our hunting place."

"But they do not hunt," Wolf told him, eager to show off what he had learned of the dark ones. "I have watched them for a finger less than a hand of days, and I have seen much of their ways, although I understand little of what they do. I do not know where they get their food, but they do not hunt for it — this I have seen. They do not even come among the trees." He hesitated for a moment, realizing this was not quite true; the girl had come among the trees that very day. However, what he said was true of all the others. "They are no threat to our hunting place," he assured Foaming Mouth Bear.

A very faint crease of anger had appeared on Foaming Mouth Bear's forehead. He had received his name because he had a temper like that of an enraged bear, always ready to explode. "That is only your judgment, Wolf. Two of them *did* come into our hunting place, did they not? If some did once, others may come again. We cannot permit it!"

An unease was growing in Wolf's mind; he feared what the chief's son and the others might have decided to do. "What is your counsel?" he asked guardedly.

"We must drive them away," answered Foaming Mouth Bear grimly. "We must drive them away from here so that they will never be a threat to us and our hunting place. If we must, we shall kill them!"

Wolf eyed the man thoughtfully. The difference in their ages didn't matter, nor did it matter that Foaming Mouth Bear was the chief's son; Wolf was a proven hunter, regarded as a man by the entire tribe, and he was entitled to voice his thoughts about anything concerning the tribe. His opinion was of as much weight as that of any other hunter. But one had to be careful with Foaming Mouth Bear.

"My counsel is that we should not do this," he said. "I have watched these people for days, as I have said, and I have never seen anything to fear from them. I think they are just people, like us, despite the color of their hair and eyes. They seem to have some magic way of getting food, and they have a magic way with animals. There have been times when the hunting was not good for us, and the Bear People were hungry. If we knew the magic way of getting food that these people have, it would be a good thing for us."

No one spoke for a moment. Then Sleek Otter said, "Do you think they might show us this magic, Wolf?"

"They might," said Wolf, "if we made friends with them."

The frown was now full on Foaming Mouth Bear's forehead. "Your counsel is foolish, Wolf! We do not know anything about these people. How could we trust them? They are too different from us — we could never be friends! No, we must treat them as we would treat a wolf pack that came into our hunting place and tried to hunt *us*. We must drive them away or slay them all!"

A chill came over Wolf as he thought of the dark-haired girl's laughter stilled by death. He glanced around at the other hunters. "Are you all agreed on this?"

There were nods and grunts of assent. Wolf saw there would be no point in trying to argue them out of their decision. He put his head down so that no one would be able to see the dismay and worry that he felt.

5

Wolf squatted beneath a tree, fingering the spear that Fleetrunner had carried here and given him, and tried to think of what to do.

His thoughts were in turmoil. Foaming Mouth Bear, after further counsel, had decided that the hunters would attack the strangers during the dark of night, setting fire to their log house and spearing without mercy any of them who tried to escape. The other hunters seemed eager and excited by this prospect, and Wolf knew that a few days ago he, too, would have been willing to kill any of these dark-haired people just as readily as he would kill a wolf or wolverine that threatened him. But the time he had spent in watching them — and the time he had spent close to the girl — had changed his way of thinking. They weren't quite strangers anymore. He would have a hard time killing the man who limped or the gray-haired woman who bossed everyone. And he could not possibly kill the girl!

It was the girl he was chiefly worried about. He grimaced with unhappiness at the thought of her trapped in the flaming log house and shuddered at the thought of a hunter's spear ripping through her body as she tried to escape. Was there some way he could save her?

He considered trying to warn the dark-haired people somehow, but his thoughts shrank away from committing such treachery against his fellow hunters, for if the farmers were forewarned, the hunters would be in danger. What could he do, what could he do?

Wolf became aware that Fleetrunner was squatting beside him. He glanced at his friend's grinning face.

"Darkness is gathering," said Fleetrunner. "We'll soon be taking care of them, eh, Wolf?"

Wolf could only nod, forcing a smile. He did not dare confide his feelings even to Fleetrunner, who had been his friend since they were little boys together. Fleetrunner would not understand.

The darkness continued to gather, the shadows thickening until the forest was as black as a cavern beneath the ground. The hunters moved close together and stared into the darkness to let their eyes grow accustomed to it. They spoke but little, in low voices and with few words.

The scout who had been watching the strangers from the edge of the forest now joined them. "They all went inside their dwelling while there was still enough light to see by," he reported in a whisper. "For a while there were noises coming from inside, but all has been quiet for some time now. They are surely all asleep."

"Good," said Foaming Mouth Bear. "Make the fire."

Badger Fears Nothing had been crouched over a pile of tinder with a fire drill ready, and they heard a faint *whissa-whissa-whissa* as he began to twirl the drill. They were far enough in the forest that a fire's glow could not possibly be seen from the clearing. Shortly the tinder blazed up, and a man squatting next to Badger Fears Nothing quickly fed the blaze with leaves and twigs. When the fire was burning well, several men thrust thick, trimmed branches into it and held them there until they were burning well enough to remain glowing while the hunters traveled to the log house. One man carried a bundle of dry kindling to be placed against the side of the house; the men would plunge the glowing branches into the kindling. It had not rained for many days, and the logs of the dark ones' dwelling would be dry and eager to burn.

41

"Let us go," murmured Foaming Mouth Bear. "Remember, spare *none*! May the Horned One be with you all."

Silently, eagerly, they moved out of the woods and trotted into the great clearing toward the log house, a dark shape huddling beside the stream, which glowed faintly with reflected moonlight. Wolf moved along with the others. What can I *do*? he fretted. Shall I yell out? Could I pretend that I hurt myself somehow, and made a loud noise without thinking? Would Foaming Mouth Bear and the others believe I had not done it on purpose?

The problem was taken out of his hands. Foaming Mouth Bear had not realized that the strangers might know there were other humans living in the forest. From Bright Dawn's description of her encounter with Wolf, they knew that the forest people had found them, and so they were doubly on guard against an attack. While he had been watching the dark ones, Wolf had caught glimpses of several animals moving about with the strangers. The creatures vaguely resembled wolves and made a sound like a series of loud, sharp coughs. It had not occurred to him that they might be as keen-nosed as the wolves they resembled and that their noises could serve as a warning. Now, as the hunters came closer to the longhouse, loud coughing sounds suddenly burst forth, and then a man's yells could be heard. Moments later, the longhouse's entrance was uncovered, and a throng of figures swarmed out with flaring torches. They hurled the torches in all directions, providing a scattering of small blazes that dimly lighted the area in front of the dwelling. The hunters could see that all the dark-haired ones except for the very young children were out of the longhouse, armed with weapons and awaiting them!

Wolf was elated. Now Foaming Mouth Bear's plan to take the strangers by surprise and wipe them out was impossible; the strangers were alerted and the hunters were clearly outnumbered. Wolf felt sure that Foaming Mouth Bear would call a retreat, and if no blood was spilled, there might be a chance to approach the dark-haired ones in friendship, after all.

But Foaming Mouth Bear gave a roar of rage and broke into a headlong charge at his enemies. As he burst into the light of the burning brands, his face was horrible to see, with bared teeth, contorted features, glaring eyes. He flung himself at the nearest farmer and, with a wild shriek, stabbed savagely with his spear. The farmer managed to twist away enough to avoid a killing thrust, but he howled in pain as the spearpoint tore into the flesh of his thigh. He went reeling back and collapsed to the ground, his leg welling blood that looked black in the fireglow. A deafening chorus of yells and screeches of fear and fury broke forth from the dark-haired men and women. Suddenly noise and motion seemed to be everywhere; the hunters rushed forward with savage yells to join their leader, and shrieking men and women farmers sprang to meet them!

Wolf had not joined in the charge, and he groaned to see what was happening. Things had not gone at all as he had hoped! His dream of talking with the strangers, of becoming acquainted with the dark-haired girl, had been shattered in this swirl of blood and fire. Couldn't Foaming Mouth Bear and the other hunters see that this attack was hopeless? They weren't going to be able to defeat the dark-haired ones now. Nothing would be accomplished but hurt, hate, and death!

He moved forward cautiously in a half crouch, his spear at the ready, but he did not intend to fight anyone unless he had to defend himself. He was looking for the girl.

He saw her! She stood with legs spread, gripping a wooden pole that was split at the end to form two sharp-pointed prongs — another of the stranger-people's odd tools. She looked frightened, and she was breathing hard, but she stood her ground, ready to fight.

She turned wide eyes Wolf's way, clutching her weapon. Wolf instantly stopped short, putting his arms at his sides and holding his spear point down. He wanted to make sure she understood he wasn't going to attack her. He smiled, hoping she could see his face in the faint light of the burning brands.

Bright Dawn stared at him. She recognized him, and she was ready to stick her pitchfork into his body if he should try to charge her — but it didn't look as if he intended to do any such thing. Again she was confused. Others of his kind were trying to kill her people, but this boy was standing here smiling at her as if he wanted to be friends! Was it a trick?

Suddenly a figure came lurching between her and the boy. It was Foaming Mouth Bear, his body so bespattered with blood that he looked like a spotted man in the fireglow.

Foaming Mouth Bear had lost all reason. His plan to take the dark-haired people by surprise had failed completely, and with the hunters as badly outnumbered as they were, he sensed that they would soon be driven off. He would have to lead whatever was left of them home and acknowledge defeat to his father. In his rage, he wanted to kill as many of the dark-haired ones as he could, but he had succeeded only in wounding one — the man he speared in the leg —

before he himself had been wounded when the others had closed in on him. He'd had to run from them to save his life, and that had increased his rage and shame. Now, staggering through the darkness, he suddenly found himself facing the slight figure of this girl who, he felt sure, was helpless against him. She must die by his hand to make up for everything that had happened!

Wolf saw the girl's eyes dart from him to the man towering over her, her face set in desperation. Foaming Mouth Bear thrust his spear at her, and she managed to block it with her pitchfork as she hurled herself to one side. But her foot twisted beneath her and she went sprawling. Foaming Mouth Bear took one stride toward her, his spear arm swinging up and back for a killing thrust.

Wolf had hurled himself into motion as Foaming Mouth Bear had made the first thrust at the girl, and now he recklessly flung himself in front of the man. "No!" he yelled. "You can't kill her!"

The chief's son paused to stare at Wolf. Here was a scapegoat for everything that had gone wrong. His face twisted in hatred. "You!" he roared. "It's your fault! You should have known that they were keeping watch against us!" He aimed his spear thrust at Wolf's chest.

Wolf just managed to get his spear up in time to deflect Foaming Mouth Bear's point. But the force of Foaming Mouth Bear's thrust carried the man forward, straight into Wolf's spear. Wolf saw the stone point rip into the breast of his chief's son. He saw Foaming Mouth Bear's face writhe in pain. Then the man fell backward, Wolf's reddened spearpoint pulling from his body, and collapsed in a huddle on the ground.

Wolf stared in disbelief, unable to accept that such a thing had happened. For a moment he was sure that Foaming Mouth Bear was dead; then he saw that the man's eyes were fixed on him and that his lips were moving. The boy leaned forward to catch the words.

"Snake," groaned Foaming Mouth Bear. "Wolf — snake!"

Wolf went cold. Among the Bear People the worst insult was to call someone a snake — a treacherous, poisonous creature that lies in hiding and suddenly strikes at the foot of an innocent person. To be called a snake meant that you did not deserve to continue being one of the Bear People. Foaming Mouth Bear was telling Wolf that he should be cast out of the tribe!

"I did not do it on purpose!" protested Wolf. "It was an accident. I was protecting myself! You — *you* tried to kill *me*!"

Foaming Mouth Bear ignored him and began crawling painfully toward the forest. In moments his form had merged into the darkness.

Numbly, Wolf considered his predicament. He didn't think his tribesmen were going to win this struggle. Soon they would retreat among the trees. If Foaming Mouth Bear made it to the forest, the others would find him, and he would tell them that Wolf had tried to murder him. This would make Wolf a snake in their eyes, too. It wouldn't do any good for him to try to argue against Foaming Mouth Bear; the word of the chief's son would be taken against his, he was sure. There was nothing he could do. With cold fingers of panic clutching at his stomach, Wolf realized that he would no longer belong to the Bear People. He was an outcast!

His eyes fell on the girl. She was still lying on the ground, staring up at him. She had thought herself dead when the tall, bloody man had come at her, and then the boy had saved her. She couldn't understand what had happened. Weren't the boy and the man the same sort of people? Why had the boy fought the man?

"Run away!" Wolf said to her. He gestured toward the longhouse. "Go into your dwelling. You aren't safe here."

The words were gibberish to Bright Dawn, but the

urgency of his voice and the gesture he made toward the longhouse helped her understand his meaning. She pointed toward her foot; she had sprained her ankle when she hurled herself away from the man's spear thrust. "I cannot walk," she said. "My foot is hurt."

Wolf stared at her, thunderstruck by the realization that she spoke a different language. Yet he could understand her meaning as she had understood his. He realized she could not stand up and walk.

He glanced about sharply. His finding of the girl and his struggle with Foaming Mouth Bear had taken place in just seconds, and the battle was still going on all around them. He was aware of flickers of motion and shouts and shrieks. Not far away, beside one of the guttering firebrands, was sprawled an unmoving figure, but he could not tell whether it was a Bear People hunter or one of the girl's people. He looked back at her.

"You are not safe here," he told her. "If one of my people happens by, he may kill you. I must take you away."

Still clutching his spear, he gathered the girl up, one arm beneath her knees and the other beneath her shoulders, and turned away from the battle, heading across the clearing toward the forest. The girl stiffened in fear for a moment, then relaxed. He had saved her from being killed and she realized he was now trying to keep her from being harmed by any of the other pale-haired men. She still wasn't sure what his relationship to them was or why he was trying to help her — they seemed intent on killing her and her people — but she felt she could trust him. Both times she had seen him he had seemed pleasant and friendly, and she did not think he meant her any harm. She thought he would just carry her a distance away from the battle and then help her get back as soon as there was a chance.

Behind them, the sounds of the fighting grew fainter.

Wolf was not at all sure what to do. He had to get the girl to safety, but then what? The thought that he might no longer be one of the Bear People was a grievous, worrisome thing, and he wondered if, after all, he shouldn't go to the other hunters and try to explain what had actually happened between him and Foaming Mouth Bear. His friend Fleetrunner would believe him and so, he felt sure, would most of the others. He was not a snake, and he must make them see that, despite what Foaming Mouth Bear said of him!

But . . . he considered how things might seem to them. Foaming Mouth Bear would tell them how Wolf had tried to keep him from killing the girl, and would that not seem to be a betrayal of them and the tribe? It would look as if Wolf had sided with the dark-haired ones against his own people! The hunters might even think Wolf had led them into a trap, since the dark ones had been so obviously prepared for the attack.

Wolf faltered for a moment as he suddenly realized that maybe he *had* led them into a trap! Surely the girl had told her people of seeing him in the woods. This must have been why they were on their guard. If I had not shown myself to her, he thought, they would not have expected us. The attack would have worked.

But then, he told himself, she would now be dead! All the dark-haired ones might be dead. And he would not have wanted that.

He breathed a shuddering sigh. He still did not think of himself as a snake, but he could see, now, why the other hunters might think he was. They would probably hate him. They might even come after him, seeking vengeance. He decided that he had better put as much distance between them and him as he could, while he had the chance. He would make his way deep into the forest in a direction that lay well away from this part of it. He would stay there until — he tried to swallow the sudden lump in his throat as he realized he might have to stay there, alone, forever! He could never go back among the Bear People. His father was dead and would be spared the shame of learning that Wolf had been cast out by his people, but the boy was troubled by what his mother would think. And he was particularly worried about the Horned One, for if he no longer belonged to the Bear People, was the Horned One now no longer his god?

And what about the girl? He'd had a vague notion of taking her just to the edge of the woods and then bringing her back to the log house when things had quieted down, perhaps in the morning, but he realized that he did not dare do that. He would simply have to take her with him wherever he went. Eventually, of course, he would bring her back home. Somehow he would have to make her understand this.

Bright Dawn, too, was wrestling with many worries. She was concerned that some of her people might have been injured or even killed by the pale men. She was also concerned that her mother would be grieving over her, not knowing where she was. She will think I have been carried off by the pale men, thought the girl, and then realized with surprise that this was actually what *had* happened to her!

For her, the woods were totally black, and she was badly frightened. Her only consolation was that the boy carrying her apparently was not the least bit inconvenienced by the darkness. She wondered if he could see in the dark. He did not seem to be frightened, so maybe she didn't have to be — but she was! She was also beginning to worry because he seemed to be taking her farther and farther from her home.

"Where are we going?" she asked in a soft whisper. "Must we go so far?"

"I don't understand you," Wolf told her in a normal tone of voice. He was still surprised that she should speak in a language different from his; it seemed strange that all people wouldn't use the same words for things. He suddenly thought that perhaps she was trying to tell him that she was tired and needed to sleep.

"Are you weary?" he asked, stopping. "We can stop and rest if you wish." They had come quite a distance into a part of the woods that was far from the point where the Bear hunters had gathered, and Wolf felt safe from pursuit. Even when morning came, Foaming Mouth Bear and the others would never be able to find his track.

Bright Dawn did not understand him, of course, and made no reply. He took her silence for agreement, so he gently put her down with her back against the broad trunk of an old gray oak. Then he settled himself beside her. She stiffened with fear for a moment, not sure what he intended, but quickly realized that they had simply stopped to rest for the night.

However, the terror which Bright Dawn had managed to keep in check while the boy had been carrying her along began to overwhelm her. For most of her life she had slept indoors, and even during her people's migration she had slept beneath one of the ox-drawn carts, with her mother and several others. There had always been one or two men on guard, and a comforting glow of campfires if she awoke in the darkness. Now she found herself lying in total blackness, nearly helpless because of her foot, in the midst of a dense forest where something might come at her from any direction. She clutched at Wolf. "Are we safe here?" she whispered. "What of the wild beasts?"

Wolf heard the terror in her voice and remembered the fear he had observed in the two men he had trailed through the woods, and the curious reluctance of any of the dark-haired people to get close to the trees. With a sudden leap of understanding he knew that she and they *feared* the woods, although he couldn't understand why. What could he do to help calm her fears? "Would you like a fire?" he asked, leaning toward her. "I will make you a little fire."

From the deerhide bag slung over his shoulder he took out his fire drill equipment and a handful of tinder. Shortly he had a tiny blaze going, which he quickly fed with twigs scooped off the ground.

"There," he said, looking at Bright Dawn with a

smile. "Maybe that will make you less fearful, eh? Do not worry — there is nothing to fear."

She studied him carefully in the firelight. She decided that her first impression of him, when she had met him in the woods, had been right; his face was pleasant to look at and she liked the way he smiled. She smiled back. The fire made her feel more secure, and the boy seemed so unconcerned about their surroundings that her fear began to subside. She leaned back against the tree. Before long, without even realizing that sleep was stealing over her, she let her eyes close.

They fluttered open again to look straight up at the twisted, crisscrossing gray branches and green leaves rustling slightly in a soft breeze. The light was dim, but it was obviously morning. She turned her head to look for her companion. He was gone.

Bright Dawn shot to a sitting position. "Boy!" she shrieked. "Yellowhair!" He had gone off and left her, alone and helpless, to die!

Abruptly Wolf came hurrying between two trees, looking alarmed. His face cleared when he saw she was in no danger. He grinned reassuringly. "I was looking for food," he told her. "Look what I found." He came toward her, his cupped hands spilling over with berries. "Redberries. Here — take them."

She held out her hands and let him pour the berries into them. Although she was familiar with strawberries, she had never seen berries such as these. But the sweetness of their scent told her they were edible, and she put several into her mouth.

"Ooh, they're good!" she exclaimed, and hungrily devoured the rest. She wondered if the boy's people grew these things as a crop, as her people grew grain. Was there a field of them nearby? She wished she could ask him. There were many questions she wanted to ask him, but there was no way he could answer any of them unless he knew what she was asking. Obviously she would have to teach him a real language instead of those silly words he used that didn't mean anything to her. How to begin?

She touched herself and spoke her name several times. Wolf looked puzzled for a moment, then he realized what she was trying to do. He repeated the sounds she was making and kept them in his mind. This was her name. Then he decided she might want to know his name. He touched himself as she had done, and said it.

Bright Dawn repeated it, nodding. She was glad to know his name, but she didn't want to learn his strange language; she wanted him to learn hers. She held her hand toward him and tapped it with her finger. "Hand," she said.

And so they spent the rest of the morning, Bright Dawn pointing at things and speaking her words for them, and Wolf listening carefully and trying to commit everything to memory. Near noon he made her understand that he had to go seek more food for them. He saw that she was nervous about being left alone — she could not go with him, of course, because she couldn't walk — so he tried to show her, with gestures and facial expressions, that she would be quite safe while he was gone. The only creatures that might be a danger to her, wolves, did not venture out during the day, and most others, catching her human scent, would simply avoid her. But to make her feel better, he gave her his spear to clutch while he was gone.

Despite the spear, Bright Dawn was fearful while Wolf was gone and intensely relieved when he returned after a few hours, carrying the limp body of a large brown-and-black-speckled bird which he had shot with an arrow. She watched with interest as he plucked its feathers, cleaned it, spitted it on a trimmed branch, and began to roast it over a blaze he kindled with his fire drill. She had never eaten any meat but that of the goats, when one or two of them were slaughtered for a special feast day, and she found roasted woodcock delicious. Wolf had also filled his leather waterbag from a stream he had found, so they were able to slake their thirst.

Bright Dawn regarded Wolf with approval; he was obviously a capable, self-reliant person. Ploughmaker and Starwatcher had explained that the pale-haired forest people were hunters, but Bright Dawn hadn't quite understood what that meant. She had pictured the forest dwellers running about after scurrying animals, trying to seize them with clutching hands. Surely anyone who had to depend on sheer chance for their food must often be hungry. But now she could see from Wolf's ways that hunters possessed skills and knowledge that made their food-getting far easier than she had thought. None of her people could have found food and drink in the forest so easily as Wolf had found them.

They spent the rest of the day with more language lessons. This became the pattern for the next few days while Bright Dawn's ankle gradually mended. Wolf hunted food for the two of them, and the rest of their time was spent learning more about each other and slowly becoming able to converse. While Wolf taught the girl a few words of his language, he recognized that they needed one common tongue and concentrated on learning her language rather than trying to teach her his. Thus, by the time Bright Dawn was beginning to be able to take a few hobbling steps, she and Wolf could talk together a little.

"I must return to my people, Wolf," she told him one evening after they had eaten. "My mother surely thinks I am dead. She must be grieving. I want to spare her that, as soon as I can."

He understood well enough to nod. "We go when Bright Dawn walk well," he said awkwardly in her language. "Wolf take Bright Dawn to place of home." He hesitated a moment, then said, "We no more be together, Bright Dawn."

She eyed him thoughtfully. "What will you do when I go home? Return to your people?"

He made a rueful grimace. "Wolf no more belong to people! When Wolf fight Foaming Mouth Bear to save Bright Dawn, Wolf"— he groped for a way of making her understand —"Wolf no more have people. People not want Wolf now."

She stared with stricken eyes, understanding for the first time what his saving of her life had cost him. But an idea suddenly burst upon her like a torch blazing out of darkness. "Oh! Wolf — you can join *my* people! They will be glad to have you because you saved me from death. You can live with us. We shall teach you how to grow grain and you can teach us how to hunt!"

He considered her words with excitement that quickly grew to match hers. He had resigned himself to the fact that he could never rejoin his own people, but being with Bright Dawn had helped him avoid thinking about the loneliness of living by himself for the rest of his days. He would not have to face that loneliness if he belonged to her people, even though they were not ones he had been born among. It would be a new, exciting adventure to become one of these strange people, making their ways part of his life. It would also be greatly satisfying to be able to stay with Bright Dawn. He nodded, eyes shining. "We go to Bright Dawn's people when Bright Dawn walks well," he promised, "and Wolf will stay with Bright Dawn's people!"

7

"You mean that you worship an *animal*?" asked Bright Dawn in a voice tinged with both astonishment and derision. Her ankle was fully healed, and she and Wolf had started out on the return trip to the place of her people. For the first time since they had become able to talk with each other, their conversation had turned to religion, and both had been astounded to learn that the other's deity was different.

"Horned One not animal," Wolf protested. There were times when he wished she had learned his language instead of the other way around; it would certainly make it easier to explain things! But he did the best he could. "He is like man, but have beauty and forest ways of animal." He looked at her accusingly. "You say 'animal' like that is low, worthless thing! Animals our *brothers*!"

"Brothers? You kill them for food," she pointed out.

He shrugged. "That is just way of things. They kill each other for food, too. But when we kill animal, we ask of it forgiveness for taking life of it. We remind it we must kill to live. That is way Horned One made things to be."

"Your Horned One did not make things," said Bright Dawn a trifle tartly. "The Mother did!"

Wolf shook his head. "I not understand this 'Mother' of yours. You say she is earth? But earth not person, it"— he swept his arm in a gesture that took in the forest around them —"it is *place!*"

"It is a place, yes, but the Mother's spirit is everywhere within it," Bright Dawn explained. "It is the Mother who makes the earth bring forth growing things. She makes the grain sprout in the fields, and the green grass rise in the meadow, and the leaves of the trees burst forth and turn green."

"What of cold, white time, then?" Wolf demanded. "Why things not grow then, if Mother so powerful?"

"In wintertime she has grown old and lost most of her power," Bright Dawn acknowledged. She went on, drawing upon the things she had been taught since childhood. "But just when she is so old that she would die, if she were like you and me, she is reborn and becomes a young girl again. That is when spring happens.

Then, as she grows older and becomes a woman, spring turns into summertime. She is at her most powerful in autumn, when she makes the earth give forth its harvest, so that our people will have food for the winter. But after harvest she grows older and her power becomes less. That is when winter comes. But we know that she will always be reborn again."

Wolf stopped in his tracks, eyeing her with amusement, and she, too, stopped and turned to face him. "You mean this happens over and over, and that is why there is a greening time and a warm time and a fall-of-leaves time and a cold, white time?" he asked. Then he snorted derisively. "That is not way of it at all! I will tell you what really happen. Horned One —" He broke off and turned his head quickly. From somewhere in the forest nearby came a sudden explosion of sounds — sounds of anger and strife.

"A bear," said Wolf in his own language. "And a man. We must go help!"

He broke into a run, moving in and out among the trees, heading toward the sounds, Bright Dawn scurrying at his heels. Suddenly they burst upon a scene that made the girl stop short in terror.

In a small space among the trees a man crouched with his back against a tree trunk, trying to fight off the attack of an enraged bear. He was a small man, and well past middle age, with hair and a beard of frosty gray. He was breathing heavily, using a spear to fend off the slavering bear's rushes, jabbing at the creature's face. His left arm was welling bright blood from three gashes that a swipe of the bear's taloned paw had opened up.

The bear was not particularly large, but reared up on its hind legs, poised to bat at the man, it was taller than he and just as tall as Wolf. To Bright Dawn, who had never seen a bear, the creature seemed a demon. Its teeth were bared, its mouth was foaming, and it was snarling continuously. It kept lunging at the man, and it was clear that he would not be able to hold it off much longer.

Wolf leaped forward, brandishing his spear and shouting in his own language. Bright Dawn wondered why he didn't just shoot the beast with an arrow. He appeared to be taking a dreadful chance in challenging such a fearsome thing with only a spear. But Wolf had no intention of killing the bear if he could possibly avoid doing so, for even though he was an outcast from his tribe, he had been reared as one of the Bear People, and this animal was sacred to him. "Ho, brother, do not fight me," he yelled at it. "Spare this man. He is not food for you! Think of the salmon in the stream, think of the honey in the hollow tree. Give up this fight, I beg you, and we shall all live!"

At the sound of his voice the bear had turned, snarling, and dropped to all fours to face him. It wavered for a moment, uncertain whether to charge this new adversary or turn back to the one it had been fighting. Then the idea that it was outnumbered — and in danger — seemed to seep into its animal brain, and its rage began to subside. It licked its lips with a red tongue and abruptly whirled to lumber off among the trees, growling.

Wolf knew that it had given up because it recognized him as kin and did not wish to harm him, and he knew it would not return. He put down his spear and bent over the man, who had collapsed at the foot of the tree and lay gasping for breath. The man, who studied the boy with pain-filled eyes, was clearly a forest dweller; his eyes were blue and there were still glints of gold in his gray hair and beard, but Wolf had never seen him before. He was dressed like the boy except that his tunic was sleeveless — the wounds inflicted by the bear were in full view. Wolf regarded them for a moment, then looked toward Bright Dawn.

"Stay with him," he said in her language. "I must find something."

"What if the monster returns?" she quavered.

He looked puzzled for a moment. "Oh, the bear? He will not bother us now. He knows you are my friends." He vanished into the forest, leaving her staring in wonderment at his words. She turned to look at the man, who seemed to be regarding her with confusion. He said something in a questioning voice, but she shrugged and shook her head to show that she did not understand.

Wolf was back shortly, with a cluster of glossy brownish leaves in one hand and a mass of something white and gauzy in the other. Bright Dawn realized this was a wad of cobwebs; not the broken, dirty cobwebs one sometimes had to clean out of an overlooked corner of the longhouse, but fresh, dew-cleaned cobwebs the boy had gathered from the broad silken sheets that a certain kind of spider spread with great abundance on the forest floor. Kneeling beside her, over the man, Wolf first rubbed the leaves vigorously between his palms, crushing them so that they gave off a strong aromatic tang. Then he pressed them onto the bloody claw marks and molded the swaths of cobweb over them to hold them in place. The man watched this operation with obvious approval, and said something. Wolf looked at him in surprise.

"What is it?" asked Bright Dawn.

"I can understand him," said Wolf. "He speaks like Bear People, but — different, some ways. I think because he not like either of us, he not speak like either of us, but he speak like me, only little different."

Bright Dawn nodded. She did not think it strange that everyone living in the forest would speak much alike. "What does he say?"

"He want us to take him to his dwelling." Wolf helped the man get to his feet, supporting him with an arm around his back. The man leaned against him, cradling his wounded arm with the unhurt one.

"This way," the man said with a grunt, jerking his head toward the right. They moved off slowly, Bright Dawn picking up Wolf's spear and the man's, and keeping a step behind.

"I am called Wisdom Seeker," the man told Wolf. "I am grateful to you, hunter, for saving my life. I was not hunting the hairy-man-of-the-woods, but he was in great anger over something when I encountered him and sought to take my spirit. He would have, but for you."

"I am glad that we were near and could help," said Wolf. "I am Wolf, of the Bear People, and the girl's name is Bright Dawn."

"She is not like us," remarked the man.

"No, her people have come from a far place, and

make their home at the edge of the world. Their ways are different — they do not hunt, but get their food out of the ground in some way."

Wisdom Seeker glanced back at Bright Dawn with interest. "Ah! I would learn of her people and their ways! But she does not speak our tongue at all, does she?"

"No, but I can speak her tongue, a little," Wolf told him proudly. "I could tell her of your words and then tell you of hers." He eyed the man sidelong. "Are you a hunter of your tribe? What are your people called?"

"I do not have a tribe. I left my people, long ago, to live alone."

Wolf stared. Here was one like him, who had no tribe! But this man had left his tribe by choice, not because he had to. "Why do you want to live alone?" he blurted.

Wisdom Seeker chuckled, then winced, holding his injured arm. "I cannot live among others," he said. "I seek to walk the spirit path."

"Ai!" Wolf made the sound that expressed reverent awe among his people. From the look on his face, Bright Dawn could see that the man had told him something impressive.

"What did he say, Wolf?" she pleaded.

"He is a —" Wolf floundered; he did not know the

words for magic or magician in her language. "He is one of power! One who speaks with the spirits!"

She understood his meaning, and she, too, looked at the gray-haired man with respect. Among her people, only the three women who represented the Mother had the power to perform magic. But Bright Dawn was aware that things were very different among the forest folk, and she presumed their magicians were all men.

They had traveled no more than a few hundred paces in the direction Wisdom Seeker had indicated when they entered a tiny clearing and came upon what was obviously the magician's dwelling, a hut made of branches and earth, built around the bole of an enormous oak tree, which stood not far from the bank of a small stream. A patch of bright sunlight colored the ground around the hut, and Wisdom Seeker eased himself to a sitting position within it, his back against the hut's wall. For a moment he studied the couple who stood side by side, looking down at him. Then he spoke to Wolf.

"Stay the night with me. I have food in plenty. I would talk with you and learn more of this strange girl and her people. I wish to repay you for saving me from death."

Wolf shrugged. "There is no need for payment. But I will see if Bright Dawn is willing." He turned to the girl and spoke in her language. "He want us stay with him. If we go on now, we be at place of your people by sundown. If we stay here for night, we be there by midday tomorrow. It is only little longer time, Bright Dawn."

Bright Dawn was anxious to reach her home and let her mother know she was alive and well, but she could see that Wolf wanted to stay. As a matter of fact, so did she; she was curious about the magician. "It is only a little time longer," she agreed. "Let us stay."

8

"Tell me of yourselves," urged Wisdom Seeker as they sat before his hut in the twilight after their meal. "I know you are a hunter of the Bear People, Wolf; you told me that. But what is Bright Dawn's tribe, and where did they come from? How did you and she find each other? What do you seek together?"

Wolf looked at the ground. "I am not really a hunter of the Bear People anymore," he said in a low voice. It still pained him greatly to think of this. "I will tell you all that happened."

Wolf spoke of everything that had taken place since he and his friend Fleetrunner first saw the two strangers near the Bear People's camp. Wisdom Seeker listened carefully and watched the boy and girl intently as the firelight gleamed on their young faces. At times he interrupted with questions, mainly directed at Bright

Dawn, which Wolf translated for the girl. When Wolf reached the end of his account, telling of his hope to become a member of Bright Dawn's people, Wisdom Seeker sat looking into the fire for a time, saying nothing.

Finally he looked up. "Wolf, from what you have told me, and from Bright Dawn's answers to my questions, it is easy to see that her people hate and fear our world. Do you think you can be happy living with such people? Can you learn to dig in the ground instead of striding among the trees? Can you turn your back upon the Horned One and worship this Earth Mother Bright Dawn speaks of?"

Wolf's face took on a stricken look. "I . . . I don't know, Wisdom Seeker. I must try, I think! I *must* have a tribe! I must belong to someone. And"— he glanced at the girl beside him —"I have found that I want to be wherever Bright Dawn is."

The man nodded slowly. "Ask Bright Dawn if she feels sure her people will accept you," he directed. "What if they should hate you, Wolf, because your people attacked them? What if they refuse to let you join them? Ask her what she would do then."

As Wolf translated the magician's words, Bright Dawn's face, too, became twisted with doubt. Such thoughts as he was voicing had entered her mind, but she had pushed them out, refusing to consider them. "No," she protested, looking at Wolf. "They will honor you because you saved me. I will tell them you are not like the other pale men. They will accept you. They must!" Tears welled in her eyes, sparkling in the firelight.

"No, no," said Wisdom Seeker soothingly. "Tell her not to cry, Wolf. Tell her I will ask the spirits to reveal what the future holds for you and her, if she wishes."

"Bright Dawn," said Wolf, looking at her anxiously, "do not cry. He is going to speak with the spirits to find out what will happen to us!"

Sniffling, Bright Dawn looked toward the man with interest. He pushed himself up off the ground and went into the hut, stooping to make his way through the low entrance. He emerged a few moments later with a pair of small leather bags in his hand and a drum tucked beneath his uninjured arm. The drum was formed of wide strips of birch bark glued together with tree sap to make a circle over which a piece of deerskin was stretched. Wisdom Seeker settled himself by the fire again, with the bags at his side and the drum in his lap.

He put a hand into one of the bags and drew out a quantity of dried leaves. He rubbed these between his fingers, crushing them to a coarse powder which he sprinkled onto the little tongues of flame flickering over the glowing branches of the fire. At once, a thick, gray, pungent smoke flew upward.

Wisdom Seeker began to tap on the drum with his fingertips, a slow, steady beat he accompanied with a wordless humming. Bright Dawn found that her vision was becoming slightly blurred. The darkness around her seemed to be wavering.

"Bright Dawn," said a low voice beside her. Wolf was seated next to her, but the voice had come from the other side. She turned to see who was there, but there was no one. Frightened, Bright Dawn clutched at Wolf's hand and felt his fingers close reassuringly around hers.

"Wolf," said a voice behind the boy. He twisted, craning his neck, but saw nothing.

Wisdom Seeker's head was thrown back and his eyes were closed. Instead of humming, he began to sing. The boy and girl were startled by the voice coming from his mouth; it was not his. It was a very different voice, the voice of another man.

> *Boy who has no tribe,*
> *Girl with hair the color of night.*
> *There is a bond between you.*
> *You will stay together.*

Wolf turned to look with surprise at Bright Dawn, and she looked back at him. The voice had sung in the language of the forest people, and she did not know what it had said, but the look in Wolf's eyes made a timid smile flutter at her lips.

The voice sang again:

> *You go to seek a tribe.*
> *The way seems short, but it will be long.*
> *The way seems easy, but it will be hard.*
> *The way seems sure, but it is not.*
> *Yet you will find your tribe.*
> *You will put two old things together*
>   *to make a new thing.*
> *And your tribe shall prosper!*

Abruptly there was silence, as the chant and the drumbeat ended. Wisdom Seeker remained as he was for a few moments, head back and eyes closed. Then he sighed, opened his eyes, and leaned forward, working his shoulders as if they had grown stiff. "The spirits have revealed what lies ahead for you," he said softly. "So shall it be."

"What did he say?" Bright Dawn begged, looking at Wolf. "Whose voice was that? What did *it* say?"

"I think it must have been a spirit voice," said Wolf, awed. "It sang that . . . that there is a bond between us, Bright Dawn, and that we shall stay together!" He watched anxiously to see how she would react to this. Her eyes widened and she smiled. Reassured, Wolf went on. "It sang that we would have a long, hard time returning to your people. I do not understand that, for there is less than half a day's journey left. But it sang that we would get there. Then it sang something else I do not understand. That we would take two old things and make a new one that will make the tribe prosper. I cannot think what that means." He looked at the magician and switched to the forest tongue. "I did not understand all that the voice said, Wisdom Seeker. Do you?"

The man shook his head. "That is the way the spirits reveal things, Wolf. You will understand what was meant when the time comes."

"Now let me show you something," he said. "Another thing of magic." From the other leather bag beside him he took a gnarled, dull black stone. "Take it and hold it so," he told Wolf, holding the stone between thumb and forefinger, so that a length of it protruded. "Strike it hard against the blade of your spear — like this." He showed what he meant with a quick motion of his hand.

Wolf took the stone uncertainly, holding it as directed. He picked up his spear and held it with the stone blade over his lap. Then he struck the blade with the stone in the way that Wisdom Seeker had shown him. Both he and Bright Dawn gave exclamations of surprise, for as the black stone struck the gray one, a spray of tiny, fiery points of light shot in all directions and instantly vanished.

"It is a Firestone," Wisdom Seeker told them. "There is fire locked within it! Strike it against the stone of which spear and arrowpoints and knife blades are made, and it throws out tiny bits of fire. Make a pile of dry leaves and strike the stones together so that the fire bits fall among the leaves, and they will set the leaves ablaze. I found that stone and another in a part of the forest where there had been a great fire, and there was a pit, as if a giant fist from the sky had struck a blow there! It was a place of magic, and the Firestones are things of great magic. I would have you keep this Firestone, Wolf. It is the greatest gift I can give you."

"Thank you, Wisdom Seeker," said Wolf, examining the stone with awe. "This is a great gift indeed!"

"Not as great as the gift of life you gave me, man of the Bear People," the magician told him. "Had you not come to my aid, that hairy-man-of-the-woods would have slain me!"

He yawned hugely. "Ah . . . I cannot stay awake as you young ones can. I must sleep." He glanced at Bright Dawn, then back at Wolf. "I have seen that

Bright Dawn is not yet used to the forest, Wolf. She might feel safer sleeping in my dwelling. You and I can stay out here by the fire."

Wolf translated his words for the girl, who smiled thanks at the elderly magician. She bade Wolf good sleep and entered the hut, where a pile of furs against the wall formed a bed for her. It was, indeed, more comfortable than sleeping on the ground, as she had been doing since she and Wolf had come into the forest. But even so, it was a long time before she could get to sleep. The questions the magician had asked her earlier kept thrusting into her thoughts, and she had to admit to herself that she did not really know how her people would feel toward Wolf. The words the spirit voice had sung did not give her any comfort, for they seemed far from clear. Her mind a tangle of uncertainties, she finally fell asleep.

9

Wolf cleared his throat nervously. "We shall soon be there," he remarked.

"Good," murmured Bright Dawn. She studied him with sidelong glances. It was obvious that something was on his mind. Ever since they had left Wisdom Seeker earlier that morning, Wolf had been darting looks at her but saying little. Several times he had apparently been on the verge of telling her something but had changed his mind. She was wondering if perhaps he was getting ready to say that he did not want to join her people after all. If that were so, she was not sure what she would do.

At that moment, Wolf made up his mind to do what he had been trying to do since they had left the magician. He stopped and turned to face the girl. He cleared his throat again. She faced him, her heart beating faster.

"Bright Dawn," he began, "we shall soon be among your people. There is something I must know before we get there. It is about — about what the spirit voice sang of last night, when it sang that there was a bond between us and we were to stay together." He paused and looked anxiously into her face. "I was glad to hear the voice say that! Does it . . . does it make you glad, too?"

"Oh, yes!" she told him.

His face burst into a smile. "I wasn't sure. The spirits play tricks sometimes, it is said." Then his expression became serious again, and he fumbled at the pouch that hung from his belt, where he kept small possessions. "Bright Dawn, among my people when a man and woman decide to stay together, the man gives the woman a gift. I have no gift to give you except the magic Firestone that Wisdom Seeker gave to me." He took it from the pouch and held it out to her. "I pledge myself to you, Bright Dawn," he said formally.

Bright Dawn did not want to take such a valuable thing from him, but she felt she must; she could see how important it was that she accept it. "Thank you, Wolf. It is a wonderful gift!" She hesitated a moment, not quite sure what she should do. It seemed to her that she should say something special, as he had, so she echoed his words. "I pledge myself to you, Wolf." It was not at all the way her people did this sort of thing, but that did not matter in the least now. She and he could have it done the right way later.

They walked hand in hand for a time, content to say nothing. Soon they saw the brightness ahead that signified the large clearing the farmer people had made.

"We are nearly there," Wolf said. "You know, Wisdom Seeker actually lives quite near your people, Bright Dawn — less than half a morning away. Perhaps we could visit him sometimes."

"I would like that," she told him.

They stepped out from among the trees and beheld the place of the People. They were a good mile or more from where Wolf had been when he first saw the farm settlement, and it looked different to him. A thin gray thread of smoke was rising from the opening in the longhouse roof. The field of grain was golden in the morning sunshine. There did not seem to be anyone at work yet.

"What is that?" said Wolf, stopping suddenly.

In the center of the field of waist-high grain stood a tall structure that had not been there before. It was a pole with a bundle of some sort affixed to the top of it.

Things seemed to be hanging from the bundle, as if it had arms and legs.

"That is a scarecrow," Bright Dawn told him, shielding her eyes to peer toward it. "When the grain begins to ripen, the rooks and crows come to feed on it, so we put up a figure in the shape of a man, made of plaited straw and bits of oxhide, to frighten them off." She frowned as she continued to look toward it. "But that does not look like —"

"It is not a thing of straw and hide," said Wolf grimly, interrupting her. He broke into a run. Her heart filled with foreboding, Bright Dawn sped after him.

Halfway there, she heard him give a wail of anguish. He doubled his speed and in moments stood before the thing, staring up at it with shock-filled eyes. The dead body of Fleetrunner hung from the pole. Strips of oxhide bound him to it, so that his arms and legs dangled and his head hung forward, chin resting on his chest. His body was rent with more than a dozen puckered spear wounds, and he was covered with a blackened crust of dried blood. His eyes were red, gouged-out pits. A mob of flies swarmed buzzing around him.

"It is one of your people," said Bright Dawn in a whisper. She was shocked almost to the point of numbness. The boy had been blinded, tortured, and hung up to die, and she could not believe that her people would have done such a thing. Jolly old Haybinder, who was always making jokes; good-natured Morningstar, who plaited straw dolls for the little children; *her own mother* — could *they* have let this happen, watched it, helped do it? A sob wrenched her throat. Dimly she realized that the dogs were barking in the longhouse and had been for some time.

Wolf turned toward her. She took a step backward when she saw the look on his face.

"I cannot do it," he said through gritted teeth. "I cannot live among the people who have done this to my friend! I do not want to be one of them! I hate them! I spit on them! I would kill them all, if I could!"

She burst into tears. Her, too? Did he hate her? Did he mean that he wanted to kill her, too?

They were both so shaken by their emotions, the boy with grief and hate, the girl with terrible sorrow, that they were caught unawares. Alerted by the dogs, the farmer people had seen the boy and girl coming, and several of the men, crouching as they ran and hidden by the waist-high grain, had surrounded them. Now they leaped out of hiding and attacked Wolf, beating him with wooden clubs until he sprawled, unconscious, among the grain. One of the men seized Bright Dawn.

"No!" she shrieked, struggling. "Don't hurt him!"

"Bright Dawn!" exclaimed the man, recognizing her for the first time. He let her go, and she rushed to kneel beside Wolf, sobbing. The men exchanged surprised glances.

"We thought you had been carried off," said one. It was Ploughmaker. "Your mother and all the rest of us grieved for you. But maybe you weren't carried off, eh? Maybe you went willingly!"

He seized her by the hair, jerking her upright so that she screamed with pain. "Some of our people have been *killed*, Bright Dawn! Starwatcher is dead! Old Rain Dancer is dead. The pale ones lurk at the edge of the forest and send their little shooting-spears at us if we come too close. We are at war to the death with them — and you have been playing in the woods with one!" He shook her so that her teeth rattled and, seizing her by the wrist, began dragging her toward the longhouse. "Bring the pale one," he directed.

Two of the others picked up Wolf by the shoulders and feet and carried him along after Ploughmaker and Bright Dawn. Wolf's head lolled, and Bright Dawn saw that there was blood in his hair.

She sobbed. She had been so hopeful that the People would accept Wolf because he had saved her and cared for her. She had pictured smiling faces and friendly voices. Never had she dreamed anything like this could happen, that there could be such resentment toward her and hatred for the boy she cared for — hatred great enough, she suddenly realized with horror, to turn him into a blood-spattered corpse like the one hanging in the field!

10

As Bright Dawn, the unconscious Wolf, and their captors neared the longhouse, people came swarming out and rushed toward them. One of the women stopped short, stared in disbelief for a moment, and then let out a joyful shriek. "Bright Dawn!"

"Mother!"

Ploughmaker reluctantly loosed his grip on the girl's arm, and in moments she and her mother were hugging, laughing, crying, and trying to ask questions and answer them all at once.

"Where have you been? I thought you were carried off by the pale ones! I feared you were dead!"

"I was nearly killed. But that boy saved me. He took care of me. Oh, mother, don't let them hurt him!"

As the meaning of her daughter's words cut through her joy, the older woman stepped back and stared at

Bright Dawn. "You were saved by one of the pale ones? He *helped* you? How? What happened?"

Bright Dawn and her mother were now the center of a crowd, including even the three Wise Ones, pressing about them to congratulate the girl on her return and to find out what had happened. She saw a chance to save Wolf while there was still time.

"Listen to me, all of you," she begged, raising her voice. "This pale-one boy who came with me — he saved my life! When one of the other pale ones was going to kill me, this boy fought him and saved me. I hurt my ankle and could not walk, and he carried me into the woods so I would be safe. He has been taking care of me until I could walk again. Please, please, don't hurt him! He is not our enemy. I told him he could join us and become one of the People."

By the time she had finished, the crowd had grown so silent that the sound of the wind rustling the tasseled grain tops could be heard. Bright Dawn turned slowly, staring at the faces around her, hoping to see that her plea had made everything all right, that the People now understood about Wolf. But she saw only expressions of disbelief and growing anger. Her mother's face alone had a look of understanding and compassion and, it seemed, a touch of wistful sadness.

"You told him he could join us?" asked an elderly

woman named Bird of Spring. "His people killed my man, Rain Dancer!" Tears began to roll down her weather-beaten cheeks, and her face twisted in sudden anger. "I would rather die than let such a one live among us! I want to see him up there with the other!" She flung out an arm to point at Fleetrunner's corpse suspended over the gently waving grain. There were murmurs of assent from the crowd.

"No!" shrieked Bright Dawn. "You cannot do that! You must not!"

"It is not for you to tell the People what they cannot do and must not do," admonished Cloud of Summer, the middle-aged member of the Wise Ones. "That dead one in the field is there as a warning to the others of his kind. Two dead pale ones would be an even stronger warning."

"No," sobbed Bright Dawn. "No!"

Cloud of Summer eyed her for a moment, frowning, then turned to Bright Dawn's mother. "I think she cares much for this pale one, Birdsong."

"Perhaps," said Bright Dawn's mother guardedly.

"You need not say 'perhaps' — yes, I do care for him," Bright Dawn announced in a defiant voice. She hesitated, then blurted, "We are pledged to each other!"

There were gasps, and a contemptuous snort from

Ploughmaker, out beyond the crowd, where he stood over Wolf's prone figure. Cloud of Summer was flanked by the young girl and the elderly woman who were the two other Wise Ones, and all three were regarding Bright Dawn with bleak faces. Her mother's face was expressionless.

"You have pledged yourself to an enemy of your people," said Snow Walker, the oldest Wise One, in a voice like stones grinding together.

"I tell you, he is not an enemy!" cried Bright Dawn. "He is not like the other pale ones. He does not even belong to them anymore. He was cast out of his tribe when he fought one of them to save me!"

"He fought for you because he was attracted to you," Cloud of Summer told her. "You told us how he approached you in the forest, when you went to find the goat. He had been watching you. But if he had not seen you, he would have been trying to kill others of the People just as all the pale ones were doing. He is *our* enemy even if he is not yours, Bright Dawn."

"It is not true that I would have fought any of you, then," Bright Dawn heard Wolf say. She peered through the crowd and saw that he was sitting up, holding his head with one hand, glaring up at the farm folk who had turned to stare at him as if he were a dangerous wild beast. Ploughmaker and another man stood close by, holding their spears ready to stab if he should make a sudden move.

"I would not have fought you, *then*," Wolf repeated sullenly. "I even tried to keep the others from attacking you. I was not your enemy then. But I am now! I am because of what you did to my friend, Fleetrunner."

"He was your friend, eh?" said Ploughmaker, and prodded him with the spearpoint, just hard enough so that a tiny red bead of blood oozed out of Wolf's cheek. "Well, then, we shall let you be up there with him." A look of surprise came over his face, and he glanced toward Bright Dawn. "How is it that he can speak a real language? The other one couldn't."

"Wolf, Wolf," moaned Bright Dawn. Now they would kill him for sure, she knew. With his angry words he had destroyed whatever chance there might have been for them to accept him as a friend.

"Shall we kill him, then, and put him with the other?" Ploughmaker asked of Cloud of Summer. He braced his legs and drew back his spear, sure of her answer.

But she hesitated. "I do not think so, yet," she said after a moment. "If he can speak both his language and ours, he may be of use to us. He may be able to tell us things about his people that could help us fight them. I think we should let him live for a time, while we see what we can find out from him." She looked at first one, then the other, of the Wise Ones on either side of her. "Do you agree, sisters?"

Blossom, the youngest, gave a single nod. The other, Snow Walker, said, "We must be sure that he cannot run away. He must be penned, as the goats are penned."

"We could bind him and keep him in a corner of the longhouse," Blossom suggested.

"I will not have him in the same house with me!" squalled old Bird of Spring. "I will kill him if I get the chance!"

"We could keep him out here, tied to the goat pen," said Ploughmaker. "Whoever is standing guard during the night to watch for an attack by the pale ones could keep an eye on him. He wouldn't get away."

"That might be best," Cloud of Summer agreed. She looked at Wolf. "Do you understand, pale one? We are going to let you live." Wolf shrugged and said nothing.

Bright Dawn fought to keep from showing the wild joy and relief she felt. She had thought she was going to see Wolf stabbed to death before her eyes, and now, suddenly, he was safe.

But Cloud of Summer was watching her intently. "Do not rejoice, girl," she said in a low voice so that Wolf couldn't hear. "I shall only let him live until he tells me all that I want to know. Whatever he did for you, whatever he *is* to you, he is still *our* enemy, and he is going to die!"

They tied Wolf's hands tightly behind his back, then they looped the end of a long leather thong around his neck and tied the other end to one of the wooden stakes that formed a corner of the goat pen. Wolf submitted as if he didn't care what happened to him. He smiled wanly at Bright Dawn.

"The spirits tricked us after all," he said to her. "They said we would get back to your people, but they didn't tell us what an unhappy thing it would be."

"But they said that the tribe would prosper because of us," she protested. "They made it sound as if everything would be all right!"

"Tricks," he said, and sighed. "Just tricks." He dropped to a sitting position against the rails of the pen.

"Come away, Bright Dawn," her mother said in a soft voice. "The others do not like it that you stay here and talk to him."

Bright Dawn could see that most of the people were watching her with anger and contempt. Somewhat to her surprise, she realized that she didn't care. But she feared they might take out their resentment on Wolf if she seemed to be defying them. She kept her face impassive as she followed her mother to the longhouse, but she was frantic with worry and self-reproach. It was *her* fault that Wolf now faced death; she had urged him to come here and assured him that he would be welcome. Did he hate her? She couldn't bear the thought, but she could understand if he did.

They entered the longhouse and made their way down the narrow hallway. This was all a familiar sight to Bright Dawn, and one that she had longed to see while she had been in the forest. Now she felt like a stranger.

"Are you hungry?" her mother asked in what seemed an unnecessarily loud voice. "I can make you some gruel. Come."

Hunger was the last thing on Bright Dawn's mind, but she sensed that her mother wanted to get her into their cubicle, away from the rest of the people. That suited her. She ducked past the woven hanging, letting it swing back into place behind her.

Birdsong dropped to a sitting position on the mat that served as a bed and motioned her daughter to sit close to her. She brought her lips close to Bright Dawn's ear.

"Daughter — you do care greatly for the pale-one boy, don't you?" she said in a soft voice.

Biting her lip to keep from crying, Bright Dawn nodded.

Birdsong sighed and nodded, as if this were the answer she had expected. "What is he called, this boy?"

"Wolf."

"Wolf," repeated Birdsong, stumbling over it a bit. It was a word from the boy's language and meant nothing to her; the People's word for the animal was very different. "This Wolf — how did he take care of you when you were in the forest together? Did you have enough to eat?"

"Plenty, always," Bright Dawn told her proudly. "Food such as we never have here! Sweet red berries and good-tasting roots of plants, and the roasted meat of forest birds and animals. Wolf is a great hunter!"

"But you say he has no tribe — that his people cast him out. Where did you stay, then, if no longhouse was open to you? Where did you sleep?"

"We slept on the ground, beneath the trees, most of the time," said Bright Dawn, forgetting her troubles briefly enough to smile at the astonishment her words produced in her mother's expression.

"But what of the wild beasts and evil spirits?" protested Birdsong, thinking of the tales Ploughmaker and Starwatcher had told of the shining eyes and strange sounds they had experienced in the forest at night.

"Wolf is not afraid of those! Why, he drove off a terrible monster that was attacking a man we met.

95

It was a furry thing, bigger than a tall man, with red eyes and many sharp teeth. Wolf made it run away! But, anyway, there are not many such creatures in the forest. That was the only fearsome thing I saw in all the days I was with Wolf. Mostly there were just birds and little gray tree-dwellers with long, bushy tails."

"You were safe and comfortable and happy with him, then?" Birdsong asked, looking at her daughter intently.

"Oh, yes," the girl assured her.

Birdsong gnawed her lip thoughtfully. "For days after you disappeared, I grieved," she said. "I thought never to see you again. I feared you had been carried off to be hurt and killed by the pale ones, who seemed like evil spirits to all of us. I cried and cried! Then, this morning — oh, how astounded and joyful I was to see you alive and well! But I was shocked to see you with one of those pale evil spirits I hated so much. Now that you have told me how well he looked after you and how much you care for him, I do not know what to think. An evil spirit would not have saved you as he did. You could not care for an evil spirit as you care for this boy!"

She hesitated a moment, then turned her eyes away from the girl and continued speaking. "We captured that other pale one the same night you vanished. He was too hurt to be able to run away when the other ones did. And . . . we hurt him more. It was Ploughmaker's idea to hang him up on the pole to die, like the man he and Starwatcher saw hanging from the tree near the pale ones' dwelling place. It was a way of mocking the pale ones, Ploughmaker said, and of making them fear us." She put her head down. "The boy hung there for a long time, moaning. I was glad to see him suffer, for I hated him for what I thought had happened to you. Now — I am ashamed. Now that I know this other pale one saved you and cared for you, I am ashamed of what I helped the others do to his friend. Because of what Wolf did for you, daughter, I cannot hate him."

She looked into Bright Dawn's eyes. "But the others hate him, Bright Dawn, and they are going to kill him! They will put him out there in the field to suffer and die as his friend did! And if you try to prevent them, as I fear you will do, I think they would kill you, too! Their hatred of the pale ones is strong, and if they see how much you care for this pale one they will hate you, too — enough to kill you!"

"I would not care," Bright Dawn told her in a level voice. "If they kill him, I will hate them! I would not want to stay alive, among them."

Birdsong gave a tiny moan and rocked her body

back and forth with her clenched fists pressed against her chest. She leaned closer to Bright Dawn. "What if, somehow, we could help him get away, back into the woods? You would miss him and grieve for him, I know, but you would know that he was alive and safe. You would get over your grief, in time, and everything would be as it always has been."

Bright Dawn shook her head. "I would not want things to be as they always have been. I would not stay here. He would be out there waiting for me, and I would go to him."

Birdsong stared at her. "You would leave the People of your own free will?"

Bright Dawn paused to consider before answering. When she had been in the forest she had wanted nothing more than to come home. But that had been when she was sure her people would accept Wolf as one of them. Now, seeing their treatment of him and their treatment of her, everything had changed. "There is nothing here for me," she said slowly. "I can see that no one really cares for me except you. And there is no one here I really care for except you. There is no boy here who could ever take Wolf's place — there is no boy here I even like very much! I was happy in the forest with Wolf. Yes, I would leave the People. Gladly!"

Now it was Birdsong who fought back tears. "Oh —
I have regained you from the dead only to lose you
again, I think," she said in a choked voice. "But if
you go away with your Wolf, at least I will know you
are alive and happy, while if you stay here I must
watch you both die. So you must go. It is the only way.
We must help him escape, and you can go with him."

Bright Dawn's body jerked in surprise. She had not
expected her mother to be such a complete ally. "What
must we do?" she whispered with growing hope.

Birdsong shook her head slowly. "I am not sure.
But it cannot be done in daytime — there will be too
many people about. It must be done at night, when only
one guard will be near him." She thought, pursing her
lips. "You could creep out of here in the night when
all the others are asleep. It would be easy to cut Wolf
loose — I will give you a knife. But the guard is a
problem. Somehow he must be made to go away long
enough for you to set Wolf free."

"Can you help?" asked Bright Dawn.

"No, daughter, for I must stay here among the People
— it is the only life for me — and if they were to find
that I helped free their enemy, they would surely put
me to death."

Bright Dawn nodded. Frowning, she pondered how
she might deal with the guard. She thought of hitting

11

In addition to raising a large crop of grain, the People also cultivated several kinds of garden vegetables: onions, beets, and a scrawny type of cabbage that was more a loose cluster of leaves than a firm head. The owners of each longhouse cubicle had a small plot of land in which to grow their own vegetables, and Bright Dawn spent the rest of the day working with Birdsong in their garden out behind the longhouse. Many of the other women were working nearby, and while they talked and joked with one another, Bright Dawn and Birdsong were ignored. Bright Dawn understood that she had become detested by most of the People, and this strengthened her resolve to cut herself loose from them.

In the late evening, when the light was too dim for further work, all the women returned to the longhouse.

Bright Dawn and her mother made a quick meal of baked grain cakes and went into their cubicle to eat. Birdsong leaned close to the girl.

"We should not speak again, lest we waken someone. Let us say our farewells now." Her eyes brimmed with tears as she hugged her child to her. That morning she had been overjoyed to discover that Bright Dawn was alive, and now, so soon, she was going to lose her again. But at least this time she would know her daughter was alive, somewhere. "I will miss you," she whispered.

Bright Dawn, too, was in tears. "I'll miss you, too, mother! But I promise you that we shall see each other again, somehow. In the moons to come, look along the edge of the woods without letting the others see. I will put tokens there for you to find. Thank you for helping me! Thank you for being so understanding!"

For a time neither spoke. Then Birdsong said, "Here is a knife. I won't ask you what your plan is, Bright Dawn, because it will be better if I don't know. The Wise Ones will be sure to question me, and I'll just say that you must have crept out during the night when I was asleep. That will be close to the truth, and if they ask me anything else, I can truly say that I don't know."

They lay down, side by side, holding hands, listening as the sounds of activity throughout the longhouse gradually died away. At length there was silence, save for muffled snores coming from some of the cubicles nearby. Bright Dawn continued to wait for some time longer. Then she squeezed her mother's hand in farewell and slipped out into the passageway. In the cubicle, her mother silently prayed to the Mother for all to go well.

Bright Dawn had taken off her moccasins to make less noise, and with them in one hand and the knife clutched in the other, she tiptoed quickly down the passageway, past the dimly glowing embers of the cooking fires. Her heart was thudding so loudly she thought the noise might awaken someone, and she held her breath for fear that the sound of her excited breathing would be too loud. As she neared the entrance, one of the sleeping dogs perked up its ears and lifted its head to stare at her, but her scent was well known to it, so it merely wagged its tail and settled back. An instant later, Bright Dawn was outside in the night.

She sped around the area of the gardens. To her left, the river was a pale ribbon of reflected moonlight. She paused long enough to slip on her moccasins, then raced on until she reached the ox pen. She knelt beside one of the trimmed tree-branch poles that formed its corners and went to work. With the flint knife she hacked and gouged at the pole's base until she had made a small pile of shavings. To this she added the contents of her belt pouch — things she had carefully collected while working in the garden: tufts of dry grass, brittle dead leaves, anything that had seemed likely to catch fire quickly. Then, from the bottom of the pouch, she withdrew the magic Firestone.

Her plan could not have worked without this gift of Wolf's, which had been a gift from the magician, for she intended to set the ox pen afire. The twirling-stick fire-making method of her people would have taken too much time and been much too noisy. It had been Wisdom Seeker's words, translated by Wolf when the magician gave him the Firestone, that had given Bright Dawn her plan. Strike the Firestone against knife or spearpoint over a pile of leaves and the fire bits it throws out will set the leaves ablaze, Wisdom Seeker had said. Well, she would make use of this great magic right now.

She struck the stone against the knife blade as she had watched Wolf do, pointing the blade and the movement of her hand toward the kindling packed against the base of the corner pole. A cascade of bright sparks shot into the pile, and to Bright Dawn's delight and awe, one of the dry leaves caught fire at once, curling in on itself, ridden by a tiny blue flame. Bright Dawn quickly bent forward and blew on the flame so that it spilled over onto a chunk of wood and reached out to another dry leaf. She shielded the small blaze with her cupped hands and bent body until it began to spread out and lick at the gouged wood at the base of the pole. When she was sure it was strong enough to keep growing and the pole itself had begun to burn, she scooped up the knife and Firestone, shot to her feet, and began to run along the pen, away from the fire. The ox pen was next to the goat pen, where Wolf was tethered, the two forming a large rectangle. She had set the fire at the corner farthest from Wolf's guard, confident that when he caught sight of it he would run to put it out, leaving Wolf untended. The quickest way for the guard to get to the blaze was by running to his left around the pen; Bright Dawn would come the opposite way, around the right side.

She was three quarters of the way around when the oxen began to low and stamp in fear, although they were in no real danger if they kept away from the fence. But their noise served to catch the guard's attention. Bright Dawn heard a startled shout and the sound of footfalls pelting off toward the blaze, which by now had transformed the corner pole and portions of fence attached to it into strips of orange flame against the black background of the night. Bright

Dawn hurried along the goat pen, feeling her way in the dark by keeping a hand on the top rail. In a moment she became aware of a dim figure ahead, standing near the fence, looking toward the fire. Moonlight gleamed on his fair hair.

"Wolf!" she whispered. "It's me." She stretched out a hand, groping until she touched the leather thong that tethered him to the pen. She began sawing at it savagely with the knife.

"Bright Dawn!" Wolf exclaimed. "What —?"

The thong parted. "Run for the forest," she urged in a low voice. "I'll cut your hands free once we're there." Dogs were barking in the longhouse and the guard was shouting for help. At any moment people would awaken and come out.

With Bright Dawn clutching Wolf's arm so they wouldn't become separated, the two ran through the grain field, away from the growing tumult behind them. Bright Dawn exulted because she knew they were safe; no one could even see them.

Wolf came to a stop. "Careful, there are trees just ahead. Free my hands now, Bright Dawn."

She fumbled to find his wrists and carefully began to saw through the strips of leather that bound them. "That was clever of you, Bright Dawn," Wolf told her in a voice filled with admiration. "You set that fire to draw the man away from me, didn't you? But — you know, you cannot go back there now! They will know it was you. They would punish you, and I fear your punishment would be death. You are like me, Bright Dawn — you have no tribe!"

The strips fell away, and as he turned toward her she caught his hands and held them with hers. "We both have a tribe, Wolf," she said. "We shall be our own tribe! I have thought over everything the spirits said, and I know that they did not trick us after all. What they said was all true! They said we would stay together, and we are together. They said we would have a hard time before we found our tribe, and we have just had a very hard time! They said we would take two old things to make a new thing, and our tribe would prosper. And I know what they meant! You know how to hunt, Wolf, and I know how to plant things and make them grow. *Those* are the two old things the spirits spoke of!" She patted the second pouch that hung from the thong around her waist. "I brought some seeds with me — seeds of grain and cabbage and onion and beet. You can teach our children to hunt, and I can teach them to plant and harvest. You can tell them the ways of the Horned

One, and I will tell them of the Mother. We will take the two old ways of both our people and make a new way that is better. And our tribe *will* prosper!"

"I thought I was going to die back there," said Wolf after a moment. "I knew they were going to kill me, sooner or later. I had started to make up my death song." He laughed and hugged her. "Now I feel as if I have just been born!"

Together, they slipped into the vast friendly darkness of the forest.

EPILOGUE

As migrant groups of farmers reached the vast forest of ancient Denmark and began cutting into it, there were many battles between farm communities and hunter tribes, and bitter hatred simmered between the two ways of life for many years. Thousands of years later, archaeologists would find evidence of this warfare in the remains of burnt longhouses and skeletons of people who had obviously died of wounds caused by sharp-edged stone points and the heavy blows of blunt weapons.

But the archaeologists would also find evidence that, in time, the two ways of life merged, and some communities of people both hunted and planted. Perhaps this came about because young people from each kind of culture discovered that life and loving *were for more important than keeping up traditions of hatred over different ways and different appearances.*

And perhaps this is a lesson we may learn, some day.